Curious George®
AT THE LAUNDROMAT

Adapted from the Curious George film series
edited by Margret Rey and Alan J. Shalleck

1 9 8 7
Houghton Mifflin Company, Boston

Library of Congress Cataloging-in-Publication Data

Curious George at the laundromat.

"Adapted from the Curious George film series."
Summary: The laundromat becomes an ocean of suds
shortly after George arrives.
[1. Monkeys—Fiction.   2. Laundries, Self-service—
Fiction]   I. Rey, Margret.   II. Shalleck, Alan J.
III. Curious George at the laundromat (Motion picture)
PZ7.C92135   1987   [E]   87-3560
ISBN 0-395-45353-4

Printed in the United States of America.

Y   10 9 8 7 6 5 4 3 2 1

"It's time to take the clothes to the
laundromat, George," said his friend.

At the laundromat they met Mrs. Goodman, their neighbor.
"I have to wash my children's baseball uniforms,"
she said. "They have a game today."

George watched as she put the uniforms
into the washing machine.

She poured in some soap.
Then she pushed a handle and the
machine started to wash.

The man with the yellow hat started his wash, too.
"Now I can leave to do some shopping," he said.
"You wait here, George, and don't get into trouble."

George stood and watched as the clothes went
swoosh-swoosh back and forth. He loved it.

George was curious.
Could he make a machine work, too?
There was an empty machine in the corner.

He found a pile of clothes on a table
and dropped them into the machine.

He poured in some soap. First a little,
then a little more, then the whole box. He pushed
the handle and the machine started to wash.

Suds began to float right out of
the machine and over the top!

Soon, suds were everywhere!

An ocean of suds poured out into the street.

"Help! Help!" cried the owner.
"Who put all of that soap into the machine?"

"It was that monkey!" someone shouted.

People came running.
George was scared. Where could he hide?

When they reached the table,
George was nowhere to be found.

"I have to clean up this mess," said the owner.
"Everyone will have to take their clothes
out of the machines."

"That's terrible," said Mrs. Goodman. "How will I ever get my children's uniforms dry in time?"

Mrs. Goodman took the wet clothes home
and set the basket down on her porch.

As soon as Mrs. Goodman went inside,
a head popped out of the basket.
It was George!

He jumped out and looked around.
A big oak tree stood in the back yard.
The tree was tall, but not too tall for George.

He grabbed the clothes, climbed up the tree,
and hung the wet uniforms on the branches.

The sun was shining brightly,
and the clothes would be dry in no time.

When Mrs. Goodman came out of the house,
she was very surprised.
"Thank you, George!" she said.

Meanwhile, the man with the yellow hat and
the owner of the laundromat had come over.

"There you are, George," said his friend.
"You've caused a lot of trouble.
I'm taking you home."

"Wait!" cried Mrs. Goodman. "He made up for
the mess at the laundromat by hanging
the uniforms out to dry."

"Well, okay," said the owner kindly,
"but be sure to learn how to use
my machines next time, George."

When the uniforms were dry,
the children put them on.
Then Mrs. Goodman had a surprise —

a little uniform for George!